WOLF COMES TO TOWN

For Gemma, Jade, Kate, and Lucy

Copyright © 1993 by Denis Manton
All rights reserved.
CIP Data is available.
First published in the United States 1994 by
Dutton Children's Books,
a division of Penguin Books USA Inc.
375 Hudson Street, New York, New York 10014
Originally published in Great Britain 1993 by
Hutchinson Children's Books,
an imprint of Random House UK Limited
Printed in Hong Kong
First American Edition
1 3 5 7 9 10 8 6 4 2
ISBN 0-525-45281-8

WOLF COMES TO TOWN

Denis Manton

JUN 1996

Dutton Children's Books
NEW YORK

Do you like scary stories? If you don't, then don't go on.
Trust me. Because this is one of the scariest I've ever heard.
  I never knew a big, bad wolf myself, but folks around
here like to tell a story about the biggest, baddest, greedi-
est wolf of all. I don't know if it's true or not—you know
how folks talk—but this is how it goes: Once there was a
wolf who lived in the hills outside town, not far from the

stores. Now, that big wolf just loved to go shopping, but whenever he left his house he would wear a disguise, for he knew that people didn't like wolves very much. The wolf had a hundred different costumes—as I said, he loved to shop. He had suits and dresses and shirts and ties and wigs and gloves. He had a whole cupboard of shoes alone. And he had an amazing variety of hats.

This wolf especially enjoyed dressing up as a sweet old lady, a fat bearded man, or a smartly dressed young woman. When he caught the bus to town, nobody suspected who he *really* was.

Once he got to town, the wolf didn't bother to pay for any-
thing. He would go into store after store and innocently
browse around until he saw something he liked.

Then he would say, "I like it, I want it, and I'LL TAKE IT!"

He'd show his big teeth, snatch up the goods, and head home to the hills, quicker than lightning.

The wolf's house was packed with stolen merchandise:
dart boards, carpets, lamb chops, pajamas, toys, books, a
radio, and lots of ice cream. That wolf had stolen a guitar,
pots and pans, and everything else you can think of.

All day long he lay in bed, eating stolen food, drinking stolen soda pop, and laughing at his favorite cops-and-robbers shows on his stolen TV. (He always rooted for the robbers.) "This is the life," he would say. "*Woooo-eeee*, do I love this town!"

Well, it got so bad that shopkeepers were suspicious of just about everybody. One young woman with a purple hat got kicked out of three different stores just because she had a long nose...

and a fat man with a beard was shut out of every restaurant in town. He had to shave in order to eat dinner again!

One day a police officer came into an art gallery and warned the owner that the wolf had been spotted on the next block. "Better lock your doors if you don't want to lose any paintings," said the police officer. "I hear that wolf has good taste."

"Goodness gracious!" said the gallery owner, and he ordered all the tourists in the gallery to leave at once. "Get out! All of you!"

He turned and thanked the police officer for the warning.
"You can never be too careful," the gallery owner said.
"These paintings are extremely valuable—especially this
one." And he pointed to a picture of a sailing ship.

"Hmmm, yes, very nice," said the police officer, bending
forward for a closer look.

"I like it, I want it, and I'LL TAKE IT!" he snarled. And the wolf seized the painting and ran from the gallery, leaving the owner quaking with terror.

Things got more scary and more dismal. Before long, pet cats began to disappear. Some disappeared for a few days, then came home, as cats will do, but others *never* came home.

Next, small dogs began to vanish. Pet owners naturally suspected the wolf and were horrified to think that their pets might have... *might have been eaten!*

One morning, three women sat on a bench in the park. They fed pieces of bread to the ducks in the pond and pined for their stolen pets.

Mrs. Dappleberry told Mrs. Pinkwater that all three of her cats—Tiny, Ginger, and Sheba—were lost. "I miss them so much," she said. "They were such nice cats."

"Such nice *plump* cats," said the third sweet old lady, dabbing at her eye with a hankie. "Especially Sheba. But she wasn't as plump as *these ducks!*"

And when Mrs. Dappleberry and Mrs. Pinkwater looked
up from rummaging in their purses for some more bread
and a tissue, the other sweet old lady had gone. So had
all the ducks, leaving just a few feathers floating on the
pond.

On his way home, the wolf laughed and licked his lips. "I liked them, I wanted them, and I ATE 'EM!" he sang.

There finally came a day that the whole town still remembers. The Smiths had decided to have a lovely party in their backyard. But all the guests wanted to talk about was the wolf. "What shall we do?" they asked one another. "If we don't do something about that greedy wolf soon, he might start eating our children!"

"I know!" said a little boy. "Tie him up! Pull out his teeth! Handcuff him and throw him in jail!"

The boy's mother smiled fondly. "That's my son," she said. "He's very brave."

Everyone agreed that the little boy was *very* brave.

The visiting reverend patted the little boy's head. "That's the spirit, son. I like you. What's your name?"

"My name's Bernard," the boy shouted. "And I'm not afraid of a mean old, bad old wolf!"

When the light faded and it was time to go home, little Bernard was missing. He was not in the yard. He was not in the house. People brought flashlights and searched the hills, but brave Bernard had disappeared.

The townspeople searched all night, and it was almost morning before they discovered the wolf's house.

Peering in, they saw an incredible jumble of stolen clothes and toys and furniture.

"There's my clock!" a shopkeeper whispered.

"There's my carpet!" said another. "Hey!"

Everyone rushed into the house to reclaim their stolen
goods. "My dishes!" "My radio!" "My guitar!" "My TV!"
The discoveries went on and on.

"Little Bernard's little trousers!" Bernard's mother wailed, but she was pushed aside by the gallery owner as he grabbed his valuable painting.

In the bedroom, they found the wolf's disguises. There were suits, dresses, shirts, wigs, gloves, ties, shoes, and hats of all kinds.

"We'd better throw away these costumes," the mailman said.

"No, the wolf might find them," said the police officer. "Let's bury them."

"No, the wolf might dig them up," said the fire fighter. "Let's burn them."

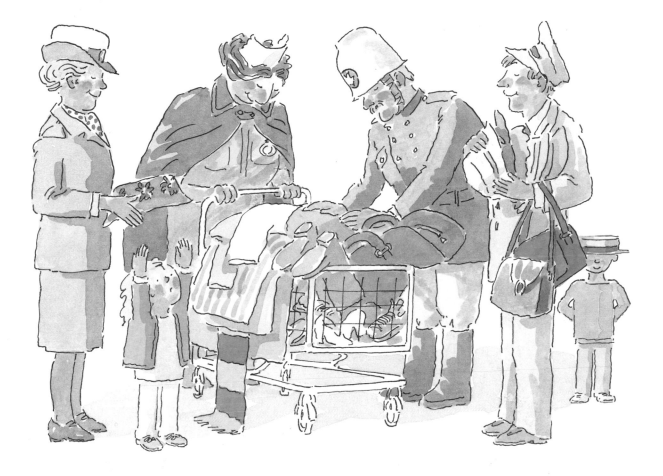

"No, that would be a waste," said the nurse. "There are plenty of poor people who need these clothes. Help me load them into this shopping cart, and I'll take them to the hospital thrift shop."

The cart was soon full, and the nurse pushed it out of the house. "They're lovely clothes," she said....

"I like them, I want them, and...
I'LL TAKE THEM TO ANOTHER TOWN!"

So the wolf did. Some folks say he got what was coming
to him from a big, bad sheriff in that new town. Some
folks say he never got caught at all. In fact, they think he
might come back someday. As for me, I'm still hoping to
see brave little Bernard again.

But that's the story. Or so they say. You know how folks
talk.